Blooming Cats

Blooming Cats

David R. Morgan
Illustrated by David Parkins

To my daughter Rebecca
(Born July 31st 1994)
Rebecca dreamed that she could fly
Like a bird-girl in the sky,
She took with her a diamond spoon
To eat the cherry-pancake moon.
D.R.M.

Scholastic Children's Books,
Scholastic Publications Ltd,
7-9 Pratt Street, London NW1 0AE, UK

Scholastic Inc.,
555 Broadway, New York, NY 10012-3999, USA

Scholastic Canada Ltd,
123 Newkirk Road, Richmond Hill,
Ontario, Canada L4C 3G5

Ashton Scholastic Pty Ltd,
PO Box 579, Gosford, New South Wales,
Australia

Ashton Scholastic Ltd,
Private Bag 92801, Penrose, Auckland,
New Zealand

First published in hardback by Scholastic Publications Ltd, 1993
This edition published 1995

Text copyright © David R Morgan, 1993
Illustrations copyright © David Parkins, 1993

ISBN: 0 590 13165 6

Typeset by Rapid Reprographics
Printed by The Paramount Printing Group

There is an old man.

Every morning and every evening
this old man walks down his street,
from the little silent house where he lives alone,
past the small row of shops,

through the park where the children have fun
and into the playground of the closed-down school
where once he was caretaker.
He goes there to feed his friends –
The Playground Cats.

There are ten Playground Cats and they all have names –

Saucy Tom, who is mischievous;

Brave Nancy,
who chases dogs;

Jolly Jacko, who loves a joke;

Fergus Frog, who can leap very big leaps;

Whoopsa Daisy, who is very very clumsy;

Nosey Norris, who is very very nosey;

Brainy Sue, who is very smart;

Enormous Ed, who is very big,

and the Tiddleywink Twins, who look the same and do everything together.

This old man spends every spare bit of money he has on food
for the Playground Cats.
At the same time every morning, every evening
the old man feeds his friends and talks to them
and every morning, every evening they make a fuss of him.

Then one morning the old man doesn't come on time.
He doesn't come all day.
Come the evening he still isn't there!

The Playground Cats are worried.

Brainy Sue says they should find out
what is wrong.

Saucy Tom says how can they do that
and gives Jolly Jacko a pinch. Jolly Jacko grins.

Nosey Norris says that he has
found out where the old man lives.

Whoopsa Daisy says they must set out at once,
trips over a puddle and squelches her nose.

So, in early evening twilight,
the Playground Cats go in a line,
through the park where the children have fun,
past the small row of shops,
down the old man's street
and stop outside his little silent house.

Fergus Frog leaps up and tries the door handle.
The door handle comes down, but the door won't budge
Nosey Norris says that the old man sleeps there.
He points with his tail to a slightly open
first floor window.
Brave Nancy says she will climb the
drainpipe to the window.

The drainpipe is old and loose and dangerous,
but Brave Nancy climbs up to the window sill.
She looks through the window.
The old man is slumped on the floor.
Brave Nancy eases the window up with
her head and jumps in.
She nudges the old man.
He is still breathing.

Racing down, Brave Nancy tells the other Playground Cats that the old man is ill.

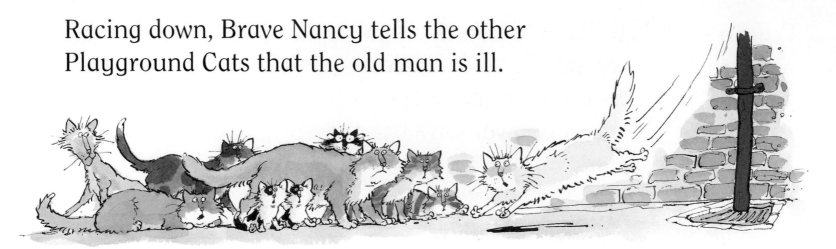

We must fetch help says Brainy Sue.

Just then, a wacky woman comes trundling along the street on her bicycle, listening to a Walkman.
Just the thing says Brainy Sue and quickly tells her plan.

Enormous Ed strolls out in the woman's path.
As the bicycle swerves The Tiddleywink Twins jump on the pedals.
Jolly Jacko jumps on the handlebars.
Fergus Frog leaps on the woman's head.
The bicycle wobbles wildly.
Whoopsa Daisy attempts a jump onto the crossbars;
She misses and catapults into the wacky woman's wobbly lap.

The Playground Cats fly off as the wacky woman and the bicycle...

CRASH

BANG

WALLOP

to the ground. Wheels spinning.

Saucy Tom grabs the Walkman and scoots.
"Oi," says the wacky woman, "Blooming cats!"

The wacky
woman springs up.

Saucy Tom gives the Walkman
to Whoopsa Daisy.

The wacky woman chases Whoopsa Daisy.

Whoopsa Daisy drops the Walkman.

Brainy Sue grabs it.
The wacky woman chases Brainy Sue.

Brainy Sue gives the Walkman
to Brave Nancy.
The wacky woman chases Brave Nancy.

Brave Nancy climbs up the drainpipe,
diving Walkman and all,
through the open window.

"Oi," says the wacky woman,
"Come back with my Walkman!"

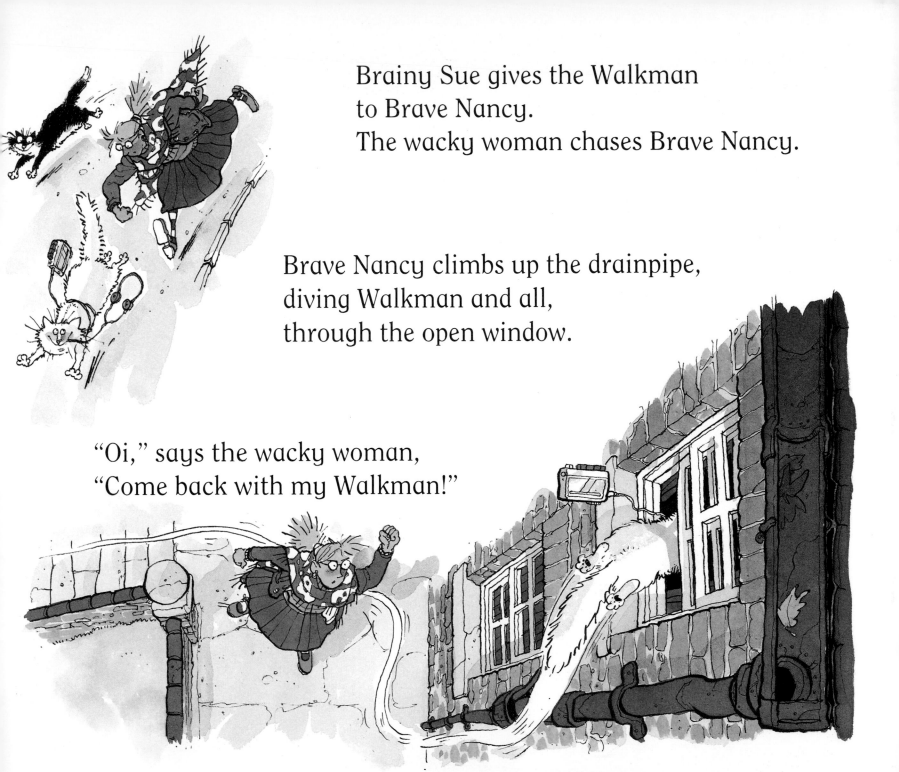

The other Playground Cats watch the wacky woman
knock on the door.
No reply.
The wacky woman opens the letter flap.
 "Excuse me," she shouts, "the cat's got my Walkman!
Is there anybody in?"
No reply.

The wacky woman tries the door handle.
The door is stiff but it opens.
"Excuse me," shouts the wacky woman,
"Is there anybody in? The cat's got my Walkman!"
"Let's go," says Brainy Sue and the Playground Cats
rush into the house. "Oi," says the wacky woman,
"Blooming Cats!"

The wacky woman chases them through the hall,
up the stairs, into the room where the old man is lying
on the floor.
The Playground Cats sit beside him.
The wacky woman, who is really a very nice lady, rushes
over to help the old man. "Well I'll be blowed!" she says,
"You cats knew what you were doing, didn't you?"

The old man gets well in hospital.
When the woman, her two children, and the Playground Cats
visit, he is very talkative and introduces his friends to the
whole ward.
The Playground Cats receive a special prize for
helping the old man.

Sometimes the woman and her two children visit the old man in his little house.
But, without fail, every morning and every evening the Playground Cats come and turn the old man's house into a playground.